Baby Brains Superstar

Simon James

WALKER BOOKS
AND SUBSIDIARIES
LONDON • BOSTON • SYDNEY • AUCKLAND

Before Baby Brains was born, Mrs Brains played classical music on headphones to the baby inside her tummy.

Mr Brains played rock and roll music on his stereo.

When Baby Brains was born,
he turned out to be amazingly clever

– especially at music. Mr and Mrs Brains were
astounded when they heard Baby Brains play his toy piano.

He could also sing
any note with
perfect pitch. Baby Brains
was a musical genius.

One evening Baby Brains said he wanted to attend
a school of music.

He started with
the tuba

but soon went on
to master the cello

and the
timpani drums.

But it was the electric
guitar that Baby Brains
loved the best.

After just two weeks the teacher said goodbye to
Baby Brains. "I can't teach you anything more," he said.

On the way home Baby Brains said,
"Rock and roll is where it's at, Mum."

Later that week
Baby Brains entered
a local talent contest.

Baby Brains plugged in his guitar and leapt about
the stage making incredible electric music.
The audience cheered and clapped.

Soon everyone wanted to hear
the extraordinary Baby Brains play his guitar.

One day Baby Brains got an important call. He was
invited to be the opening act at the biggest
open air music concert of all time.

That night Baby Brains wrote a special new song
for his first major performance –

and tried it out on Mr and Mrs Brains.

On the day of the concert Baby Brains was
measured for a special rock and roll costume

and had his
hair done
by a famous
London
hair stylist.

After giving Mr and Mrs Brains
tickets to the concert,

Baby Brains got ready.

At nine o'clock
Baby Brains was flown by helicopter
to the stadium and then …

lowered down on to the stage.

Two hundred thousand fans cheered for Baby Brains.

Everyone watched as he plugged in his guitar.

Baby Brains
looked up at the
thousands of people
sitting in the stadium.

He looked down at all
the people standing
in front of him.

Baby Brains looked
at the microphone
and mumbled
something.

"Louder!" said someone in the front row.
"Louder! Louder! Louder!" roared the crowd.

"**I want my mummy!**" yelled Baby Brains.
The crowd roared and the band began to play.

"That's not his new song," said Mrs Brains.
"Something's wrong!"

As the music blasted through the speakers
Mr and Mrs Brains fought through the crowds
of chanting fans.

"W-W-Where's my m-m-mummy?"
wailed Baby Brains as Mrs Brains
clambered on to the stage.

"I'm here!" said Mrs Brains as she lifted
Baby Brains high into the air. The crowd went wild.
It was the best performance they had ever seen.

Later, at home, Baby Brains decided to announce
his retirement from the rock and roll music scene.

And although the live recording of
"I Want My Mummy" became a huge world-wide hit,

Baby Brains preferred staying at home
listening to gentle classical music

– except of course on Fridays …

when he liked to teach rock and roll at the
children's music school.